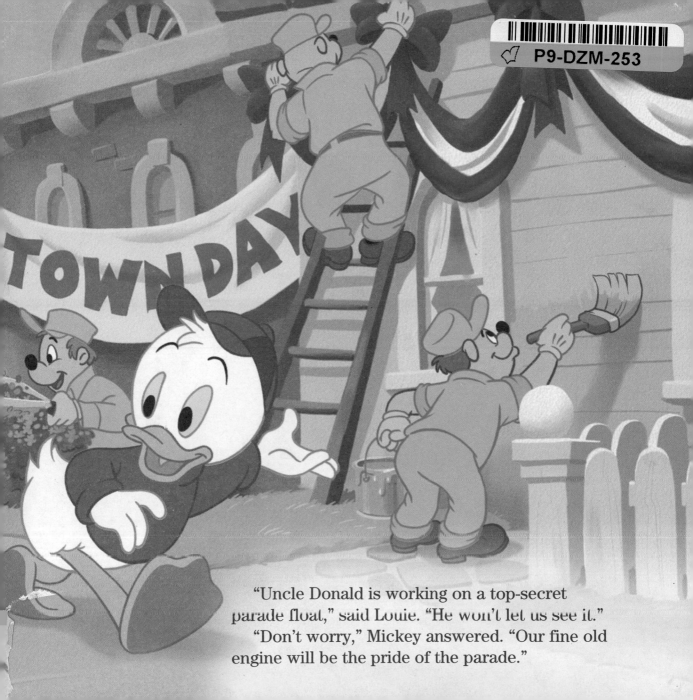

"Uncle Donald is working on a top-secret parade float," said Louie. "He won't let us see it."

"Don't worry," Mickey answered. "Our fine old engine will be the pride of the parade."

Mickey and the others arrived just in time to see their friend Goofy slide down the brass pole in the middle of the fire station.

"Hiya, gang," said Goofy.

"Goofy is a junior volunteer, just like me," Mickey told the boys as he leaned over to pat a friendly Dalmatian. "This is Freckles, the fire station's mascot."

"Here's our parade engine." Goofy grinned as he led the
boys to an old-fashioned pumper truck. "Isn't she a beauty?"
Mickey started polishing the engine while Goofy and the
boys went to work on the decorations.

"Does this truck still work?" asked one of the boys.
Mickey nodded. "Yes, it works, but it's not as fast or as
powerful as the newer engines. Now we just use it for parades."

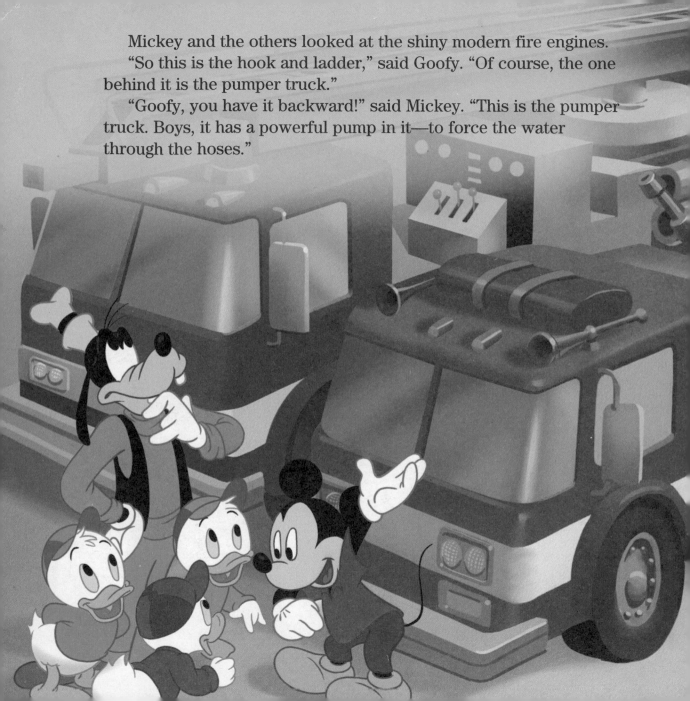

Mickey and the others looked at the shiny modern fire engines.

"So this is the hook and ladder," said Goofy. "Of course, the one behind it is the pumper truck."

"Goofy, you have it backward!" said Mickey. "This is the pumper truck. Boys, it has a powerful pump in it—to force the water through the hoses."

"It must be hard work being a firefighter," Louie said.

"It sure is," Goofy responded proudly. "Do you remember when the big hotel caught fire? We had to rescue about twenty people. I even saved Mrs. Porter's parakeet."

"Gosh, Goofy," said Mickey. "If I remember right, the regular firefighters rescued the parakeet. They just gave it to you to hold."

"But I was a big help," Goofy insisted. "I went and found Mrs. Porter and gave her back her bird."

"I'll tell you another story, boys," said Goofy. "A couple of years ago, there was a big fire in the park outside town."

"What happened?" the boys asked eagerly.

"A campfire roared out of control," said Goofy. "But I rushed boldly into the forest. That night we saved the woods from being burned to the ground."

"I remember that night," said Mickey. "It was cold.
You and I passed blankets out to the campers. I don't
remember doing much else."

Goofy looked embarrassed. After that, he didn't tell any more
stories. He and the others finally finished decorating the engine
and headed home together. Everybody looked forward to the
next day—the day of the big parade.

The whole town turned out to watch the parade. The antique truck led the way—with Mickey at the wheel. The boys were allowed to ride in the back with Goofy.

"We're going to win the blue ribbon for best parade entry," said Huey. "Uncle Donald's float doesn't have a chance."

FIRE SAFETY

Donald's float was just behind the fire engine. He had mounted a spaceship on his old pickup truck.

"Hey, Donald!" someone called from the crowd. "Is that a real rocket ship?"

"Almost," Donald answered proudly. "Get a good look. My float is going to send the judges to the moon."

Donald drove his wobbly rocket on down the street, sparks flying everywhere.

Suddenly, the rocket caught fire. Within
seconds, the whole float was in flames.
"Help!" squawked Donald. "Fire!"

"I'll save you!" Goofy cried. As Mickey pulled to a stop, Goofy
jumped off the fire truck. He grabbed one of the hoses and hooked
it to a nearby hydrant. Then Goofy began spraying Donald's float.
Before long, the fire was out.

Goofy was a hero at last. During the award ceremony after the parade, the mayor asked him to come forward.

"Goofy, you were the pride of the parade," said the mayor. "I'd like you to accept this blue ribbon for bravery. In fact, you're the bravest junior volunteer who ever held a hose!"